Brownies

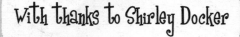
With thanks to Shirley Docker

STRIPES PUBLISHING
An imprint of Magi Publications
1 The Coda Centre, 189 Munster Road,
London SW6 6AW

A paperback original. First published in Great Britain in 2009
Published by arrangement with Girlguiding UK
Brownie logo, uniforms and badges copyright © Girlguiding UK
Text copyright © Caroline Plaisted, 2009. Illustrations copyright © Katie Wood, 2009

ISBN: 978-1-84715-103-2

A CIP catalogue record for this book is available
from the British Library.

Printed and bound in the UK.
2 4 6 8 10 9 7 5 3 1

Brownies

Sleepover Surprise

Stripes

Meet the Brownies

Katie

Katie, Grace's twin, is super sporty and likes to play games and win. She wants to get every Brownie badge and her Six is Foxes!

Jamila

Jamila's got too many brothers, so she loves Brownies because NO BOYS ARE ALLOWED! Jamila is a Badger!

Ellie

Awesome at art and crafts, Ellie used to be a Rainbow and likes making new friends. Ellie is a Hedgehog!

Animal-crazy Charlie has a guinea pig called Nibbles. She loves Brownie quizzes and Pow Wows. Her Six is Squirrels!

Charlie

Grace

Grace is Katie's twin sister and she's ballet bonkers. Grace enjoys going on Brownie outings, and she is a Rabbit!

Chapter 1

The Badenbridge Primary School hall was buzzing with excitement! It was Tuesday night and, after an action-packed evening of fun, the Hedgehogs, Foxes, Badgers, Rabbits and Squirrels – the Sixes that made up the 1st Badenbridge Brownies – were all sitting in the Brownie Ring. Vicky and Sam, the two unit Leaders, had called a Pow Wow.

Pow Wows were when the Brownies got together to think of ideas for brilliant things to do. Best friends Charlie, Ellie, Grace, Katie and Jamila grinned at each other from around the circle.

Vicky smiled. "OK, girls. Can anyone remember a special thing that the First Badenbridge Brownies do at this time of year?"

Some of the Brownies, especially the newer ones, looked puzzled. But Lauren, the Sixer of Hedgehogs, waved her hand enthusiastically.

"Is it something to do with Thinking Day?" she asked.

"Good suggestion," said Sam, "but we've already had Thinking Day for this year. Anyone else got any ideas?"

Ashvini, the Squirrels' Seconder, put up her hand. "It's the sleepover!"

"Yesss!" Some of the Brownies cheered.

"A sleepover?" exclaimed Charlie and Ellie at the same time.

"That's right!" Vicky declared. "The First Badenbridge Brownies' Annual Sleepover is coming up!"

Ellie, Grace, Katie, Jamila and Charlie giggled with excitement. They already knew that being a Brownie was great fun, but a Brownie Sleepover? That was just brilliant!

Jasmine, who was in Badgers with Jamila, put up her hand.

"Does that mean it's time for our show too?" she asked.

A show? The best friends couldn't believe it. A sleepover *and* a show?

"What happens at the show?" asked Grace. Grace was mad about ballet and had recently performed a routine with the other girls from her dance class. Another show, especially with all her new Brownie friends, sounded like a great idea.

"All sorts," Sam replied. "The Brownie Show is your chance to reveal your many talents. And we know Brownies have lots of them!"

"Yes," said Vicky. "Can any of you remember some of the performances in last year's show?"

"I read a poem," said Lucy, who was a Rabbit with Grace and Charlie's sister Boo.

"Some of us put on a play about Brownies," added Bethany, who was a Squirrel with Charlie.

"And some of us sang, and there was some dancing," added Caitlin, who not only went to the same ballet class as Grace, but was also in Rabbits with her.

"It was brilliant, wasn't it?" said Vicky.

"Yes!" called out all the Brownies who had taken part.

"So," said Vicky, "you need to think of ideas for this year's show. You can start discussing it among your Sixes now."

Around the Brownie Ring, everyone began chatting excitedly. After a few minutes, Ellie put up her hand.

"But Vicky … when are we doing the show?" she said.

"And when do we have the sleepover?" asked Katie.

"We do them both on the same night!" said Jessica, who was Katie's Sixer in the Foxes.

"Wow!" sighed Jamila.

"Yes!" Sam grinned. "We do the show first so that your family and friends can come and see you."

"Then, when they go home, we have our sleepover," Vicky explained.

"That's brilliant!" said Charlie.

"Awesome!" agreed Grace.

"OK," said Vicky, "it's almost time to finish. There's a letter to take home with you tonight. It explains all about the sleepover and show so don't forget to collect one from Daisy before you leave."

Daisy was Vicky's daughter. She used to be a 1st Badenbridge Brownie, but was now a Guide. She came back to help out at Brownies every week as a Young Leader.

"Yes," said Sam. "Make sure an adult signs the permission slip and then bring it back with you next week. If you don't, you won't be able to stay overnight!"

"Now, girls," said Vicky, "go and collect all your things together and then come back into the Brownie Ring to sing 'Brownie Bells'."

Ten minutes later, Grace, Ellie, Charlie, Jamila and Katie had letters in their hands and were gathered outside with their parents, ready to go home.

"A sleepover!" exclaimed Katie.

"And a show!" Jamila grinned.

"I can't wait," declared Grace.

"Nor me," agreed Charlie and Ellie excitedly.

Chapter 2

Next day, at lunchtime, the friends were sitting in the playground.

"I love sleepovers!" said Ellie.

"Me too," agreed Charlie. "And just imagine a huge one with all the Brownies! Food, fun, giggles – and Brownies as well!"

"Plus a show!" declared Grace. "I'd love to do a dance. Perhaps with Caitlin!"

"That'd be brilliant," said Jamila.

"Do you think everyone does really amazing things?" Ellie wondered aloud.

"What do you mean?" asked Katie.

"You know," said Ellie. "Do you think they're all great at singing and acting?"

"I expect some are," Jamila said, "but that doesn't mean everyone will be. Brownies is about having fun and doing your best – that doesn't mean we have to be the best."

"Course not," said Grace. "Why are you so worried about it, Ellie?"

"Oh – I'm not…" Ellie replied. "Well, actually, I kind of am."

"Why?" asked Jamila, concerned for her friend.

"Because I hate getting up in front of other people and acting and stuff!" exclaimed Ellie. "I was even nervous about making my Brownie Promise at the Promise Celebration!"

"It didn't show," said Charlie. "You did it perfectly. It was me who forgot the words!"

"Well, if you really don't want to sing or dance, you don't have to," said Jamila.

"But if it's a show," sighed Ellie, "what else is there to do but go on stage?"

"Hmmm…" Grace murmured.

Ellie had a point, and none of her best friends knew what to say.

The five girls were still talking about the show later in the week.

"I'm going to ask if I can play the keyboard," said Jamila, a keen musician.

"Cool," Charlie replied. "Do you think I can do something about animals?" Animal-mad Charlie wanted to be a vet one day.

"Why don't you ask Vicky at the next Brownie meeting? She said to come with ideas," suggested Grace.

"Don't forget we have to see what the other girls in our Sixes want to do," Katie pointed out. "We can't decide without talking to them about it."

"Good point," said Jamila.

"Yes," said Ellie. "I think we'd all better wait until Brownies before we absolutely, definitely make up our minds…"

The girls did so many after-school clubs and activities that they didn't see much of each other out of school that week. But they met up at the weekend to go to the cinema. Afterwards, they went for tea at Jamila's. They were all so excited about taking part in their first Brownie Sleepover and Show that they couldn't stop talking about it! So it was a good job Tuesday night came round quickly.

The Brownie meeting got off to a prompt start, soon after the five friends arrived. Vicky gathered everyone together in the centre of the hall and waited for quiet.

"Tonight, girls, I've got happy and sad news all rolled into one," she said. "You all know that Jessica has recently had her tenth birthday."

All the Brownies nodded. Jessica was the Sixer of the Foxes, and they particularly remembered her birthday because she had brought loads of yummy cakes to Brownies that day.

"Well, she has been along to Guides to see what happens there," Vicky went on. She smiled at Jessica, who blushed at all the attention. "And she'll be moving up to Guides in a couple of weeks. Our sleepover will be her last night at Brownies."

"Aww," all the Brownies sighed.

"We'll be saying a special goodbye to Jessica during our sleepover," said Sam. "And we'll be asking some of the older Brownies to share their memories of Jessica's time with us."

"But we don't want her to go!" declared Sukia, one of the younger Brownies. "We want her to stay here with us to have lots more fun!"

All the other Brownies laughed. But they knew what Sukia meant. Jessica was everyone's friend. It was hard to imagine Brownies without her.

"I know," said Vicky kindly. "We'll really, really miss Jessica, won't we? But we won't be losing her completely. She'll still be part of the guiding family."

"Yes," said Sam. "We'll see her at special outings and maybe Thinking Day celebrations.

And she'll always be part of the Brownie Friendship Circle."

"I'll be coming back to see you soon anyway!" said Jessica. "My cousin is joining Brownies next term and I'm going to bring her on her first night!"

"That's great," said Sam.

"Come on, Brownies." Vicky grinned. "Let's all give Jessica a special Brownie clap before we get on with our meeting!"

Chapter 3

After the special announcement about Jessica, the Brownies went into their Sixes to talk about the show.

"Last year we did a play," Boo, Charlie's older sister, told the other Rabbits at their Six table.

Molly, their Sixer, grinned. "It was really good fun. We wrote it together."

"What was it about?" asked Grace, who was amazed at how clever the Rabbits had been not only to perform the play, but to write it as well!

"It was a funny one about Vicky and Sam," Boo explained, giggling. "We did

loads of jokes about them getting ready to take us on an outing."

"And about Brownies getting everything wrong," laughed Molly. "Like turning up at the wrong place – and at the wrong time!"

"So what should we do this time?" wondered Caitlin. "Another play?"

"I think it'd be good to do something different," said Molly.

"So what are we all good at?" asked Boo. "What do you all like doing?"

"Dancing!" said Grace and Caitlin at the same time, before collapsing into giggles at their jinx.

"I like singing," said Lucy. "But I quite like dancing too. Except I'm not that brilliant at it."

"Course you are!" said Molly. "I remember seeing you at the school's Christmas disco – you were amazing!"

"Hey!" said Grace. "Why don't we do a routine to something in the charts?"

"Yeah," said Boo. "Then we could sing *and* dance. Cool!"

"I like it," said Molly. "What do the rest of you think?"

Caitlin and Lucy liked the idea a lot.

"That's sorted then," said Molly. "Now all we've got to do is choose the song and start learning it!"

Over at the Squirrels, Vicky was talking with the Brownies about what they might do.

"So you don't fancy doing a song," said Vicky.

"And we definitely don't want to do a play," added Megan, the Sixer.

"Do any of you play instruments? Or have an interesting hobby, like cheerleading?" Vicky wondered aloud.

"I entered the school poetry competition last year," Bethany said. "I read a poem and got a certificate for it!"

"Oh, I remember that," said Vicky. "Didn't you do that as part of your Entertainer badge?"

"Yes!" Bethany smiled proudly, looking down at the badge on her sash.

"I've got a favourite poem about dogs and cats," said Megan.

"I love animals," said Charlie.

"We know!" The other Squirrels giggled.

"Well, why don't you do poems about animals then?" suggested Vicky.

"I can make a noise like a chicken," said Ashvini. "I could read out a poem about a farm and do all the animal noises to go with it?"

"*Moo*-vellous!" said Megan, and the others laughed.

"That's a great idea," said Vicky. "Do you think the rest of you would like to read or write a poem, too?"

Everyone nodded.

"Can I bring Nibbles?" Charlie asked. "He's my guinea pig and he's gorgeous. I could write a poem about him and show him to the others. He's so cute – look!"

Charlie showed them the picture of Nibbles that she had in her Brownie Promise Box.

"Ahh!"

"Hmm. I don't want to spoil your fun, but I will need to check that none of the Brownies has an allergy to animals," Vicky said. "Hang on a minute…"

She went to fetch her folder that contained the details for all the Brownies. Charlie and the other Squirrels waited anxiously as she looked down her lists.

"It's OK!" said Vicky, walking back over. "We don't have anyone who's allergic. But you must keep Nibbles in his cage." She smiled. "And I don't think it would be a good idea for Ashvini to bring a whole farmyard with her!"

Meanwhile, the Badgers had discovered that they all shared a love of music. As well as

Jamila playing the keyboard and singing, Chloe played guitar and Jasmine was learning the flute. Izzy, the Badgers' Sixer, and Holly, their Seconder, sang with a local theatre group.

"Well, it looks like you've got to form a band then!" said Daisy, who was with them at the Six table.

"Wow!" said Jamila. "That would be so cool!"

"We could call ourselves The Badger Band," Holly said.

"Fantastic," declared Izzy.

"But what are we going to perform?" Jasmine asked.

The Badgers all looked at each other. Forming a band

was an easy-peasy idea; deciding what to sing and play seemed a lot harder.

"I've got a book of easy-chord versions of top hits. Perhaps we could choose one of those?" suggested Chloe.

"Sounds great," said Jamila.

"Sorted!" said Izzy. "Badgers rock!"

Over at the Foxes, the girls had come up with millions of ideas – but kept changing their minds!

"Well, we've got to do something!" Jessica said, scratching her head thoughtfully. "It's my last Brownie Show and we've got to keep up the tradition of the Foxes being brill!"

Just at that moment, Vicky came to sit with them.

"OK," she said. "What's your idea?"

"We've got loads," Emma sighed. "But we can't choose our favourite one!"

"I know!" exclaimed Katie, suddenly having a new thought. "I got a magic set for my birthday. We could do a magic act!"

"I don't know any magic tricks," said Amber.

"Nor me," added Lottie.

"That doesn't matter," replied Katie. "I didn't know any magic tricks before I got the set. But the tricks are dead easy – and they're really good, too. There's a whole magic show list in the set. We could just follow that. And if we practise…"

Katie looked pleadingly at the other Foxes.

"Sounds good to me," said Jessica. "And I can't ever remember anyone doing a magic act before!"

"I think we should do it," said Lottie.

"And me," said Emma.

"OK – me too!" agreed Amber.

The Foxes were doing a magic act for the Brownie Show!

The Hedgehogs, on the other hand, had agreed to do a play. But as they sat at the Six table, talking excitedly about who would perform which role, Ellie was looking worried.

"What's up?" asked Lauren, her Sixer.

"Nothing…" she replied. "It's just that … I really hate going on stage. I get *so* nervous."

"Hey, don't worry," said Amy. "You don't have to do it if you don't want to."

"But I want to help you all!" sighed Ellie. "I just know I won't be able to remember any lines or anything like that."

"But you're really good at drawing and painting, aren't you?" Sukia asked.

Ellie nodded.

"Oh, I get it!" Lauren grinned. "Ellie can make and paint our scenery."

"Oh, I'd like to do that!" Ellie said. "That sounds great!"

Every Six had now decided what they were going to do at their show. What they had to do next was polish up their acts!

Chapter 4

"It's going to be brilliant," Katie declared the next morning in the playground.

"Imagine doing a show!" agreed Grace, spinning around with her arms in the air.

"I already can't wait for next week's Brownies," sighed Jamila.

"Nor me!" giggled Ellie, who was eager to get cracking with her scenery.

"Yes," said Grace. "Sam said we'd spend the whole evening rehearsing for the show.

"Told you," Katie announced. "It's going to be Brownie Brilliant!"

Waiting six days for Brownies seemed hard. But with their swimming sessions, drama classes, music groups and art lessons, the week was so busy for the five best friends that, apart from at school, there wasn't a moment to get together and catch up. Even during breaktimes, they'd been spending time with other girls in their Sixes to talk about their acts.

When they finally met up the next Tuesday, the hall was buzzing with noise. Vicky clapped her hands and called out, "Brownies!"

The Brownies quietened down.

"Phew!" Sam smiled. "We thought you'd never stop!"

"Tonight is rehearsal night," declared Vicky. "You've all decided on your acts, this is your chance to rehearse your routines!"

The Brownies looked at each other and grinned in anticipation.

34

"Vicky, Daisy and I will come round all your Sixes to see if any of you need help," said Sam. "So let's get started!"

It was an exhausting but fantastic evening – one of the best! With only two more Brownie meetings to go before the show, there wasn't a moment to waste. They'd have carried on all night if Vicky hadn't made them go home!

Over the next week, every girl was determined to make her own role in the show perfect. The Rabbits were doing a routine they'd all seen on television to a song that had reached number one in the charts. Grace spent all her spare time practising the dance in her half of her and Katie's bedroom.

Lauren and Amy had written the Hedgehogs' play, based on a story in the

Brownie Annual about the Brownie Promise.
In the first bit, the Brownies acted out
being at Brownies, so no scenery was needed.
But the other scene was set in one of their
homes, so Ellie had been put in charge of
making the stage look like it was a living
room.

Ellie decided to paint a picture of a sofa
with a telly next to it. To make the picture big
enough to look real, she'd had to glue two
huge sheets of cardboard together. But she
couldn't find a way to support the picture so
that the rest of her Six could act in front of it.
In the end, it was decided that Ellie should
hide behind her scenery, holding it up. She
was going to be on the stage after all!

The Squirrels were all busy writing their
poems, but even though Charlie had spent
ages thinking about it, and spending time with

Nibbles, she still hadn't finished hers.

"I've tried and tried," Charlie explained to Jamila, as they sat in the playground after school one afternoon. "But I can't think what to say!"

"Hmmm," said Jamila. "I suppose you want to write about why it is that you love Nibbles so much, don't you?"

"Course," said Charlie. "I just don't know how to say it."

"Why don't you write the things that you tell us about Nibbles — only do it in rhyme?"

"That's a great idea!" said Charlie with a grin on her face. "Jamila, you're the best!"

Charlie knew that she could rely on Grace, Katie and Ellie to always be her friends. But she also knew Jamila was just the best at thinking of ways to solve problems. She was so kind and thoughtful! That night, she did exactly what Jamila had suggested — and pretty soon, she'd started writing her poem.

Meanwhile, Katie and the Foxes had all worked out who was going to do which trick in their magic act. Because she was so good at playing ball games, the other Foxes had decided that Katie would be the best at doing the juggling. So every spare minute she had, Katie was throwing things in the air. At first, she hadn't been able to cope with more than two balls. But as the week went on, Katie was beginning to have a go at using three balls at the same time! She didn't always manage to catch them, but she was determined to get better.

Jamila was spending all her free time at home learning her keyboard part for The Badger Band. The Badgers had chosen to perform a recent chart hit. It sounded brilliant, but Jamila didn't want to make any mistakes, so she rehearsed in her bedroom, over and over again.

"Can't you stop that noise?" yelled Ramiz, one of her brothers, opening the door of her room and bursting in. "It's driving me mad!"

"No, I can't!" Jamila said. "I've got to get this perfect for the Brownie Show!"

"Who cares about some stupid Brownie Show?" Ramiz exclaimed. "Everyone knows that Cubs is best."

"Huh!" said Jamila, pushing her brother out of her bedroom. "Brownies is the best because there aren't any boys there!"

She carried on practising. There was no way her brother was going to stop her getting her part perfect.

At the next Brownie meeting, Vicky and Sam asked to see all the acts for the show. The girls watched excitedly as each Six rehearsed their routines, and they cheered enthusiastically when each one had ended. After the last Six finished, Vicky and Sam called everyone into the Brownie Ring.

"I am so pleased with how hard all of you

have worked," Vicky said. "You've put lots of effort into this show and I'm certain it's going to be brilliant."

"As you all know," said Sam, "next week is the last Brownie meeting before our show and sleepover on the Saturday night."

"Yeeaaaaah!" all the Brownies cried.

"So you must each take one of these letters home," Sam continued. "It contains all the final details, including what you should bring and when you should arrive."

The Brownies grinned with excitement. They all knew they were going to have the best time ever.

"And girls," Vicky said, "don't forget you've got to return the slip saying you're coming! You must have permission to stay for the sleepover. Some of you have handed this in already, but there are still some that we

haven't had back yet. You can't stay for the sleepover unless we have the signed slip!"

"I've got more permission letters if you've lost yours," said Daisy, holding the spare letters up in the air. "These are the Brownies who still need to return their slips…"

Charlie, Boo and Ellie were three of the names! Ellie knew that her mum had signed the letter, but she'd left it in the kitchen by mistake. She decided she had better put it in her Brownie Promise Box as soon as she got home so that she didn't forget it next week too. But Charlie looked at Boo, puzzled; their mum didn't forget things like that!

"Didn't you give the letter to Mum last week?" Charlie asked her older sister.

"No – I thought you'd given it to her!" exclaimed Boo. "Oh no! We'd better give it

to her tonight! Hey, Daisy! We need one of
those letters!"

Charlie and Boo gave the letter to their dad
when he came to get them from Brownies.

"Hmmm," said Dad, reading it. "Isn't
something else happening that weekend?
I'm sure—"

"But Dad, we have to go to the sleepover!"
cried Boo.

"And we're both in the show too!" said
Charlie. "We've been rehearsing for ages! We
can't not go!"

"Oh dear," sighed Dad. "I think you'd
better speak to your mum, then."

Charlie and Boo were horrified. They *had*
to go to the Brownie Sleepover and Show!
They *had* to!

Next morning, Charlie and Boo stormed into the playground looking mightily fed up.

"Disaster!" Charlie said to Jamila and Ellie.

"What's up?" Ellie asked, concerned.

"Boo and I can't go to the Brownie Sleepover and Show!" wailed Charlie, wiping a tear from her eye.

"Can't go?" her two friends replied at the same time.

"Why?" Jamila asked.

"Because we've got to go to Gran's for the weekend!" Charlie sighed. "Mum arranged it ages ago. I thought Boo had given Mum the letter about the show – you know, the one with all the dates and stuff – but it turns out that Boo thought I'd given it to her. So neither of us did and Mum didn't know it was the same date as the weekend at Gran's! Now we can't let her down."

"But you've got your poem to do. And you're bringing Nibbles!" Jamila exclaimed.

"I know," said Charlie, trying not to cry. "And I was so looking forward to the sleepover."

"Oh, Charlie that *is* a disaster!" said Ellie, but just then, she caught sight of Katie and Grace coming into the playground. And Grace was limping.

"Double disaster!" said Ellie. "This can't be happening. Look!"

She pointed over towards her two other best friends. "What's happened to Grace? She's got a bandage round her ankle!"

Chapter 5

"Grace, are you all right?"

Jamila, Ellie and Charlie rushed over.

"What's happened?" Charlie asked, forgetting her own problem.

"I did it last night," Grace explained. "I was practising the routine. I'd just got to the bit where we all jump up, I wobbled and – *crick*! I twisted my ankle!"

"She had to go to hospital and have it X-rayed," said Katie dramatically.

"Is it broken?" Ellie asked.

"No, thank goodness," said Grace. "They said I'd pulled some of the ligaments."

"Ligaments are the bits inside your body

that connect your bones and things together," Katie explained knowledgeably.

"I've got to wear this bandage and it's really itchy!" said Grace.

"But how long have you got to keep it on for?" Jamila asked.

"At least a week," said Katie.

"So you won't be able to dance in the Brownie Show!" exclaimed Jamila.

"I know," sighed Grace, tears welling up in her eyes. "And I was so looking forward to it!"

Charlie and Boo were still in a strop when
they got home from school.

"But you love visiting Gran," Mum said.

"Yeah," said Boo, "but I love the Brownie
Sleepover and Show too!"

"And I've never even had a chance to go
to the Brownie Sleepover before!" said
Charlie. "This was going to be my first one!"

"And we're going to let all the other
Rabbits and Squirrels down as well!" moaned
Boo. "It's just *so* not fair!"

Mum looked at her two daughters.

"I know you like Brownies," she said,
"but we planned this weekend at Gran's ages
ago. Long before we knew about the
Brownie Show. And we can't let Gran down.
I'm sorry, girls."

Later that night, Boo and Charlie decided to ring Gran.

"Your mum told me there was a problem earlier, Boo," said Gran. "And I've had an idea."

"What's that?" asked Boo, holding out the phone so Charlie could hear too.

"Well, we can't have you missing out," Gran said, "so *I'm* coming down to visit *you* next weekend. Then I can see you in the show!"

"Yes!" screamed Charlie, grabbing the phone from her sister. "Gran, you are the best!"

The sisters couldn't wait to tell the others their good news at school the next morning.

"I couldn't imagine going on the sleepover without you," said Jamila, hugging Charlie.

"It just wouldn't be the same!" sighed Ellie.

"Nor would the show," added Grace. "In fact it would have been a disaster with my ankle *and* you and Boo dropping out!"

"Well, Gran saved the day!" Boo declared.

"Have you looked at the list of stuff we've got to have for the sleepover?" asked Katie.

At the end of Brownies on Tuesday, Sam had given them all a list of kit to bring.

"Yes, and Mum and I are going to get a sleeping bag on Saturday," said Ellie excitedly.

"Cool!" said Grace.

"Oh, and Mum wondered if you'd all like to come round to our house for tea on Sunday afternoon," Ellie went on. "We could

get together with all our sleepover kit!"

"Go Brownies!" the others cheered.

The five best friends gathered with all their kit at Ellie's flat on Sunday as agreed.

"Let's pile all our things up according to what's on the list," suggested Katie, organizing her friends. "Then we can see if we've forgotten anything."

"OK," said Jamila. "I'll read it out."

The girls soon finished and stood admiring their bundles of sleepover kit.

"I'm so excited, I can't wait!" said Charlie.

"Our first Brownie Sleepover!" Grace said.

Jamila giggled. "I've got butterflies in my tummy!"

"That's just you feeling hungry!" Ellie laughed. "Come on – let's go and have tea."

On Brownie night, the Rabbits were upset to see Grace was still wearing her bandage.

"But you've got a solo!" wailed Caitlin.

"We can't do the routine without you!" said Molly.

"I'm sorry," Grace said sadly. "I've spoiled it for everyone!"

"Surely there must be a way that Grace can still take part," said Boo, turning to the rest of the Six.

"How?" wondered Lucy.

Vicky and Sam came over to the Rabbits' Six table. They'd been talking to Grace and Katie's mum, who'd come with the girls to drop them off.

"Your mum's just been telling us about your accident," said Vicky. "It sounds painful."

"It was," Grace nodded. "But I'm much better now."

"I'm glad to hear that," said Sam. "But what are we going to do about your part in the show?"

"I think you're going to have to sit it out and watch the other Rabbits," Vicky sighed.

"But we can't do it without her!" said Lucy.

"Yeah," said Caitlin. "If Grace doesn't do it, then I think we should all pull out."

"Oh," said Vicky, impressed by the Rabbits' loyalty to their friend.

"Well," said Boo, "it's obvious, isn't it? We'll have to work out a way that Grace can be part of it – she just won't be able to do her solo."

"Do you think I can?" asked Grace, a smile appearing on her face.

"Do *you* think you can?" Vicky asked.

"You bet!" Grace replied.

Later in the week, the five friends were chatting about Brownies in the playground.

"Do you think it's OK if I take Cuddlebear with me to the sleepover?" asked Ellie.

Cuddlebear was a toy she'd had since she was a baby. She couldn't sleep without it.

"Course!" said Jamila. "I'm going to take *my* teddy – try stopping me!"

"I can't wait for the sleepover!" said Grace. "Do you think we'll play games?"

"Boo says there'll be games and songs and

food!" giggled Charlie. "It'll be loads of fun!"

"A proper Brownie adventure!" said Katie.

At last it was Saturday night – the night of
the 1st Badenbridge Brownies' Annual
Show and Sleepover! The five best friends
joined the other Brownies putting out chairs
for the show audience. Meanwhile, mums,
dads, grans and grandads, aunties, uncles,
brothers and sisters were already beginning
to arrive!

"Can all the Brownies please put their
sleepover kit at the back of the hall?" said
Vicky, taking charge. "Then come to the
side of the stage and sit in your Sixes.
Anyone who has come to watch the show,
please find yourself a seat and sit back for
the performance!"

"Isn't this exciting?" said Jamila, hugging Ellie. "I've never been to such a big sleepover before, have you?"

"No." Ellie grinned. "But I've never been in a show before, either. I'm really scared!"

"Don't be scared," said Charlie. "Look – Nibbles is going to be in the show and he isn't worried!"

She held up Nibbles' cage; he was twitching his whiskers and looking round the room.

"He's so cute!" said Grace.

"How's your ankle?" asked Jamila.

"Loads better, thanks," replied Grace.
"And I don't have to wear the bandage any
more. I'll be fine with the new routine."

"Come on," said Katie. "Let's take our
stuff over. We should get into our places."

"OK," said Charlie. "I just need to leave
Nibbles with Georgia and Gran first."

"Hello, girls!" smiled Charlie's gran as
the best friends hurried over. "It's lovely to
see you all. And I'm really looking forward
to your show!"

"Thanks," they all grinned back.

"See you later,
Nibbles!" said Charlie,
putting down his cage
next to her little sister.

"Will you look after
Nibbles for a few
minutes, Georgia?"

"Ess!" she nodded, smiling.

Georgia, who was two, was just as excited about seeing the show as all the Brownies were about being in it.

The girls hurried over to the back of the hall with their sleepover kit. Then they joined their Sixes at the side of the stage, feeling nervous and excited. Minutes later, it was time to start.

"Right!" said Vicky. "Are we ready?"

"Oops!" said Charlie. "I've forgotten Nibbles. I'll just go and get him." She raced over to where her family were sitting.

"Oh no!" she called out. "Nibbles has gone missing! He's not in his cage!"

Chapter 6

There were gasps of surprise from around the hall.

"Don't panic!" declared Vicky, putting up her right hand.

Instantly, all the Brownies fell silent and put up their right hands too. Pretty soon, most of the audience had stopped talking as well.

"OK," said Vicky. "We're missing a guinea pig! Please help us find him!"

"But *please* don't move around without looking where you're walking!" exclaimed Charlie. "I don't want Nibbles to get squashed!"

A grown-up went over to the main door of the hall and made sure it was firmly closed. It would have been an even bigger disaster if Nibbles managed to get outside! Some of the Brownies looked in the kitchen, and others looked through all the sleepover stuff, while the adults looked under the chairs.

Charlie was frantic. What if Nibbles *had* got outside? And what if he got squashed? It was too awful even to think about. The search went on, but still Nibbles was nowhere to be seen.

Georgia, Charlie's little sister, was sitting on a chair looking round at everyone. Charlie's gran had put her on her seat and told her to be a good girl and not move while she helped look for Nibbles.

"Oh, Georgia," sniffed Charlie. "Where's Nibbles gone?"

She wasn't really expecting an answer because Georgia couldn't talk much yet. But Charlie could tell that Georgia knew something was up.

"Nib-ler!" Georgia said, smiling.

"I know!" sniffed Charlie. "I've lost him."

"No! Nib-ler!" Georgia said again.

"Can you see him, Georgia?" Charlie asked. "Is he under the chair?"

"Nib-ler!" Georgia said again, shaking her legs excitedly. "Dare!"

"Is he over there?" Charlie looked anxiously.

"Dare!" Georgia giggled, pointing her tiny toddler fingers at herself. "Nib-ler dare!"

Charlie looked at her little sister. "Dare" usually meant "there" in Georgia-talk. And she was pointing to herself.

"Have you got Nibbles?" Charlie asked her.

"Ess!" Georgia grinned. "Dare!"

She pointed to herself again.

"You've got Nibbles?" said Charlie, looking puzzled. "Gran!"

Gran looked up. "Have you found him? Has Georgia seen him?"

"Georgia – where's Nibbles?" Charlie asked again.

"Dare!" said Georgia, pulling Nibbles out from her coat as if she was doing one of the Foxes' magic tricks. "For Charlie! Nib-ler!"

Nibbles was safe!

No one was sure whether Georgia had actually taken Nibbles out of the cage or if she'd found him and was looking after him. But everyone was relieved that he was safe and the Brownie Show could begin.

Daisy introduced all the acts and the Foxes went first. Jessica, Emma, Lottie, Amber and Katie had all learned to do some card tricks, which they successfully tried out on the audience. Next, Amber made Lottie "disappear" into a cardboard box (even though some of the other Brownies thought they could see a bit of her trouser leg) and Jessica pulled a toy rabbit out of a hat. Katie had practised her juggling for hours but, in front of all the grown-ups and other Brownies, she was so nervous she dropped all

three of the juggling beanbags within her
first few throws. She picked them all up and
started again and this time she did it perfectly.
Everyone clapped and cheered when she'd
finished.

"Well done, Foxes!" Sam smiled as the
girls came off the stage. "You've got our
show off to a great start!"

Next, it was The Badger Band. They
walked on to the stage with all their
instruments. It took them a while to set up,
but then Izzy counted them in and they
played their first chord. All except for Jamila.
Her keyboard was completely silent!

Bright red, Jamila tried the chord again.
Still no sound came out. She could hear her
brothers, Ramiz and Sabir, giggling from the
front row where they were sitting with her
mum and dad. She knew something like this

would happen if they came to the show! But why wasn't her keyboard making a noise? It had worked at home earlier.

"Can I help?" Vicky asked.

"I don't know what's wrong with it," Jamila said, feeling helpless.

The other Badgers gathered round.

"Is it switched on?" asked Holly.

"Yes," said Jamila, pointing to the "on" switch.

"Is the plug switched on?" Izzy suggested.

"I'll have a look," said Vicky. "Where did you plug it in?"

Jamila's face flushed red. "Oh no! I forgot to plug it in!"

Now Ramiz and Sabir were laughing out loud. Jamila looked over at them, and saw her mum telling them off.

Serves them right! she thought.

"Sorted!" said Vicky.

Jamila put her finger on a key. It played!

"Sorry…" Jamila apologized to her Six.

"Come on then," said Izzy. "Let's rock!"

And pretty soon, everyone was clapping and tapping their feet to the beat.

Next it was the Rabbits' song and dance routine. Grace had butterflies in her tummy before they began, but she was determined not to let her Six down. Lucy and Molly took their positions on stage and then, once the music began, Grace, Caitlin and Boo came on to join them. As soon as she started to dance, Grace forgot about her nervousness. She even almost forgot about the changes they'd had to make because of her ankle! There was a moment when Lucy started to turn left when she should have gone right, and then Grace had a bit of a wobble on a turn. But in the end, they all finished with great big beaming smiles on their faces. Everyone gave them an enormous round of applause!

Then it was Nibbles' turn to make an
appearance – again! Only this time, he
twitched his whiskers from inside his cage
while the Squirrels read out their poems.
Ashvini went first and had the audience in
stitches as she read a rhyme about a farm and
made the noises of all the animals. Megan
read her poem about dogs and cats, and
Bethany did one about two elephants
going for a walk, doing the actions of their
swaying trunks. Faith had written a beautiful
poem about birds flying from country to
country as the seasons changed. Finally,
Charlie performed her rhyme with Nibbles.
He looked so cute as he gazed out at the
audience, and he twitched his nose exactly
when Charlie said how much she loved
him! You could hear everyone in the
audience say "Aaah!"

Last on stage were the Hedgehogs with their play. The audience watched as the Brownies acted out the story of what the Brownie Promise is all about and how Brownies always do their best. Ellie busied herself holding up her sofa scenery. It made the audience laugh when Amy and Sukia pretended to sit on the sofa that Ellie had painted. And when Poppy stumbled on her words at one point, Ellie, from behind her scenery, even remembered the right words and whispered them to her. Ellie couldn't believe that she'd almost done some acting on stage!

The Brownie Show was over and the audience clapped and cheered in appreciation.

"Thank you, Brownies!" declared Sam, smiling. "That was fantastic. Now, I'm sure you would all like to thank the audience for coming."

The Brownies clapped enthusiastically at their families and friends.

"And next," said Vicky, "it's time for the Annual Brownie Sleepover to begin!"

The Brownies gave a great big cheer.

"If you could all say your goodnights," Vicky continued, "the Brownies can get ready for even more fun!"

All around the hall, girls were saying goodbye to their families. Charlie gave Nibbles to her mum and dad to take home, and she and Boo waved goodbye to them, Gran and Georgia. After Grace and Katie's mum had left, they got busy helping Daisy with some games she was getting ready.

Jamila said goodbye to her mum and dad
and good riddance to her annoying brothers
and went over to help too. But then she saw
Ellie hugging her mum and could see that
she was crying. She rushed over.

"What's up, Ellie?" she asked, looking
concerned.

"She's feeling a bit
nervous about the
sleepover," Ellie's
mum explained.

"Oh, don't worry," Jamila assured her. "We're going to be here – all your best friends. And we're going to have a great time!"

Katie rushed over too.

"Come on, Ellie," she said. "We need you to be here for our feast!"

"And to help with the songs," said Jamila. "You always remember the words and I don't!"

Ellie wiped her nose on her mum's hankie and smiled.

"Sure," she said. "I'll see you tomorrow then, Mum?"

"I'll be the first one here in the morning," her mum replied, smiling. "Have a wonderful time!"

"Come on," said Jamila. "Let's see what we're going to do first!"

Chapter 7

After all the families had left the hall, the Brownies stood round, chatting excitedly with each other about the sleepover.

"Do you think we put our pyjamas on now?" Charlie asked her friends.

"But it's still quite early!" exclaimed Grace.

"Yeah – aren't we going to do some games and stuff?" wondered Ellie.

Before anyone could ask any more questions, the Brownies spotted that Vicky and Sam had put up their right hands. Quickly, the Brownies all did the same and the room fell silent.

"Thanks, girls!" Vicky smiled. "Right –
let's all gather together in the Brownie Ring
so we can let you know what's going to
happen next."

The Brownies immediately did what Vicky
asked.

"First of all, we need you to help with
getting our feast ready!"

There was a cheer from the excited girls.
They'd been asked to bring some food with
them and they couldn't wait to see what
delicious things there were to eat!

"After we've had our feast," continued
Vicky, "we'll play some games. Then we
thought we'd sing some songs and tell some
stories. Does that sound OK?"

"Yesssssss!" the Brownies replied.

"Good!" Vicky grinned. "Then let's all
help lay out the feast."

"This is scrummy!" declared Katie, reaching
for a second cupcake.

"Sure is!" agreed Jamila, who was trying to
decide what to eat next.

Spread across the tables were pizzas,
sandwiches, carrot sticks, apple wedges, crisps,
cakes, muffins and all sorts of cookies. There
were also lots of different juices and lemonade
to drink. All the Brownies were talking,
giggling and eating at the same time.

"What games are we going to play?" Ellie asked Sam as she nibbled on a slice of pizza.

"Well, the first one is a miming game," replied Sam. "It's called Charades. Have you ever played it before?"

"Not sure," said Ellie. "How do you play?"

Sam explained that you worked in Sixes and acted out, without any speaking, the name of a film, book or TV programme. The other Sixes had to guess what you were miming.

"It's really good fun," said Sam.

"Are we playing more games after that?" Charlie asked hopefully.

"Oh yes!" said Sam. "Sharks – and Doughnuts!"

"How do you play them?" Jamila wondered. She'd never heard of those games.

"Wait and find out!" laughed Sam. "Come on – eat up!"

After the Brownies finished their feast they had a quick break before playing Charades. Sam was right about it being really good fun – the Brownies kept collapsing into giggles. The Badgers did *The Incredible Hulk* and Izzy stuffed clothes inside her Brownie top to be the Hulk. She looked so funny, but no one could guess who she was!

The Hedgehogs acted out *Enchanted*. Amy was Giselle and Ellie was persuaded to be Prince Edward, even though she said she didn't like acting. But it was so much fun that she didn't mind being the centre of attention. Lauren played Queen Narissa and kept staring at all the other Sixes, pointing her fingers towards them. It was the Squirrels who guessed it in the end.

When Charades was over, the Brownies
discovered what Sharks was. It was a game
they could all play at once. Sam used a long
piece of rope to make a circle on the floor,
which became an island that was a safe place
from pretend sharks! When Vicky
called out "Stormy", the Brownies
had to run, but if she said it was
"Choppy" you had to skip.
"Raining" meant hop,

"Sunny Day" meant walk and "Windy Day" meant you had to spin around. But when she said "Sharks!" you had to jump quickly back on to the island. The problem was, Sam decided that the tide should keep coming in, making the rope island smaller and smaller. So when the sharks arrived, not all the Brownies could fit on the island. And if you couldn't get on the island, the sharks got you and you were out!

Doughnuts was just as much fun. Again the Brownies formed a circle, but this time one of the girls had to stand in the centre with her eyes shut and count to ten before clapping her hands together. Then she had to start counting all over again! In the meantime, the other Brownies had to pass a ball around the circle and, when the centre Brownie clapped, the Brownie holding the ball had to sit down. That happened over and over again until only one Brownie, the winner, was still standing up. It was such good fun.

When Doughnuts was over, Vicky put up her right hand. All the Brownies did the same and, gradually, the hall fell silent.

"Now we've got something very important to do," said Vicky. "Can anyone remember what it is?"

"Sleep?" suggested Amy.

Sam giggled. "Yes, that's later. But there's something special that we'd like to do first."

"Which is," added Vicky, "to say goodbye to Jessica."

"Awww," sighed the Brownies.

"Come on," urged Sam. "Let's form a Brownie Ring."

The girls quickly gathered together and Vicky asked Jessica to come and stand with her and Sam.

"Now," said Vicky. "Some of your Brownie friends have a few things that they'd like to say to you."

Jessica smiled as Megan, Molly, Izzy and Lauren, the four other Sixers in the 1st Badenbridge Brownies, along with Emma, who was the Seconder for the Foxes, stepped into the centre of the Brownie Ring. Each of them held a piece of paper.

"Jessica joined Brownies when she was seven," said Emma, stepping forward and reading from her notes. "She was my Brownie Buddy when I first joined and she made me feel really welcome."

Then Megan stepped forward. "Jessica has done loads of things since she's been a Brownie," said Megan. "She's worked for ten badges, and been on Brownie Camp. And she's been in four Brownie Shows like the one we did tonight."

"Four!" gasped some of the younger girls.

"I went on a Brownie unit Holiday with Jessica last summer," said Molly, smiling at her friend as she spoke. "Jessica was really brave because she got a spider out of the shower for me. And she was also really kind to me when I was feeling homesick."

"Aaaahh!" sighed the Brownies.

"I went on a Brownie Adventure Day
with Jessica," said Izzy. "There were
Brownies, Guides, Beavers, Cubs and Scouts
from loads of different units there. It was
great. We played cricket, we held owls, we
helped make a gigantic camp fire and we got
to do archery. We also had the chance to do
a climbing wall, and I wasn't sure if I wanted
to. But Jessica told me I could do it, and she
climbed the wall at the same time as me.
And I was really glad I did it because it was
fantastic fun – and my brother wasn't brave
enough to do it with the Cubs!"

All the Brownies laughed when they heard
that. Then, finally, Lauren stepped forward
to speak.

"Jessica is funny, kind and brave and
really good fun," she said. "We're really glad
you've been a Brownie with us, Jessica.

We'll miss you – but the Guides are going to get a great new friend."

"Yeaaaaaay!" agreed all the 1st Badenbridge Brownies.

"Thank you, girls," said Sam. "That was really lovely. I think all of us understand how you feel about Jessica. We've loved having her with us. So, Jessica, we'd like to present you with this special badge."

Vicky smiled. "This badge is to thank you for being a Brownie and doing so much at the First Badenbridge Brownies."

Sam gave the badge to Jessica, who

blushed and grinned from ear to ear.

"Thanks!" said Jessica.

"It's also for you to take with you to Guides," said Vicky. "You can wear it on your Guide clothes to show the others that you've been a Brownie. Well done, Jessica."

And all the Brownies clapped and cheered.

chapter 8

When Jessica's special presentation was over, Daisy asked the Brownies to stay in the Ring to sing.

"I'm going to teach you all some of the action songs that we sing at camp!" she explained. "Can the Brownies who've been on unit Holiday help me explain what the actions are, please?"

Six of the older Brownies, including Jessica, of course, stood up. The other Brownies watched eagerly as they began to sing the first song and perform the actions.

"This is brilliant!" Jamila giggled as she stood up with her friends and started to join

in with the first song: "Head, Shoulders, Knees and Toes".

The Brownies didn't think they'd ever laughed so much or had so much fun as they went on to sing "One Finger, One Thumb" and then "If You're Happy and You Know It". They couldn't stop laughing as they tried to keep up with the music, words and actions.

When the singing was over, it was storytime.

"I never thought we'd do so much in one evening!" said Charlie.

"Me neither," agreed Ellie. "Last time I went on a sleepover with my friends at my old house, we just watched DVDs, talked and fell asleep. We even forgot to wake up for our midnight feast!"

Vicky told the first story, and then Sam suggested the Brownies make up the next

story themselves. She made up the first line,
about two Brownies who were doing a good
turn one day, and Vicky made up the next
one. Then, one by one around the Brownie
Ring, each girl had to suggest what happened
to the two Brownies next. Everyone had
really brilliant ideas and the story got funnier
and funnier. Finally, the story got back round
to Sam. She looked up at the Brownies as she
said the last line, and caught a bunch of them
yawning.

She smiled. "Well! It looks like you're all
worn out! You'd better get your sleeping
bags sorted. Then get your pyjamas on and
clean your teeth."

"Quick!" Katie said to the others. "Grab
your sleeping bags! Then we can make sure
we all sleep alongside each other!"

The girls raced to fetch their things.

"How about we put our stuff down there?" Ellie suggested, pointing to the other side of the hall.

"Good idea," Jamila agreed.

The five friends unrolled their sleeping bags and laid them out in a row. Then they put on their pyjamas and joined the queue to wash their faces and brush their teeth.

Ten minutes later, the girls were all tucked up in their sleeping bags. "I'm too excited to sleep," sighed Charlie as she snuggled down with a fluffy toy guinea pig that she always took to bed with her. He was called Nibbles Two and looked just like the real Nibbles.

"Me too!" said Grace, stifling a yawn.

"It doesn't look like it!" Katie giggled and then started to yawn herself.

"Has everyone been to the loo?" Vicky asked. She was standing in her night stuff, next to the light switch by the door, with a torch in her hand.

"And do you all know where your torches are?" Sam asked.

All the Brownies checked and said they did.

"Well then," Vicky said, turning off the

lights. "Sleep well, Brownies! See you in the morning!"

Soon, the hall was completely quiet. Outside, the rain fell heavily on the pavement. Grace, Katie, Charlie, Jamila and Ellie had thought they'd still chat after lights out, but they were so tired, they soon began to snooze. Well, Grace, Katie, Charlie and Jamila did. Ellie, snuggling Cuddlebear, just couldn't. The excitement of all the games had stopped her from thinking about home. But now everything had calmed down, Ellie was feeling sad again. She wished that she was tucked up with Cuddlebear at home.

Ellie heard someone cough, so she knew she wasn't the only one who was still awake. She hugged Cuddlebear closer and squeezed

93

her eyes tight, listening to the rain and the gusts of wind that were swishing through the trees.

Then she heard it.

Waaaaa!

What was that?

She heard it again. It was a wailing noise; like someone singing badly.

Ellie peeked out of her sleeping bag. Was one of the Brownies still awake and singing? The hall was quiet.

I must have imagined it, Ellie thought.

But then the noise started again – and this time it went on for a while!

Waaa! Waaaaa!

"Charlie!" Ellie whispered, grabbing her friend's shoulder.

At first Charlie didn't stir, but Ellie kept shaking her until finally she said, "What is it? What's up?"

"There's a noise!" hissed Ellie. "Listen!"

Slowly, Charlie sat up, feeling chilly after the cosiness of her warm sleeping bag.

"It's just the wind. I can't hear anything else," she said, rubbing her sleepy eyes.

"Go back to sleep, Ellie!"

Waaaaaaaaaaa!

"Argh!" cried Charlie, now wide awake, "What was *that*?"

"Exactly!" whispered Ellie. "I'm scared! Katie! Jamila! Grace! Wake up! There's something scary in the hall!"

Ellie leaned across to all her friends, shaking them awake.

"What's going on?" said Katie sleepily.

"There's a noise!" said Ellie tearfully.

"Don't cry, Ellie," said Jamila, getting out of her sleeping bag and climbing across to comfort her friend. "It's all right. There's just a bit of a storm outside, that's all."

Waaaaaaaaaaaaaaaaaaaaaa!

"It's a ghost!" shrieked Grace.

"Shush!" said Katie.

"Wassup?" Molly asked.

Waaaaaaaaaaaaa!

"Eeek! Vicky! Sam! Help! What's that scary noise!" cried Molly.

Within seconds, all the Brownies in the hall were wide awake and, like Ellie, they were all terrified of the noise.

"Shush, shush, Brownies!" soothed Vicky, shining a torch around the dark hall. The only other light was coming through the windows from the street lights outside.

Waaaaaaaaaaaaaaaaaaa!

"It sounds like it's coming from over by the window," said Sam. She grabbed her torch and went over to investigate.

Waaaaaaa!

The scared Brownies leaped out of their sleeping bags and huddled together with Vicky in the centre of the hall.

"It's coming from outside," Sam reported.

"I'll go and take a look." She opened the hall
door and stepped out into the lobby. The
Brownies heard the sound of the main school
door being unlocked.

Waaaaaaaaa! The noise was getting
louder!

"Well I never…" said Sam, shining her
torch out into the rain.

Chapter 9

Sam stepped out into the dark and rainy night. The door closed behind her.

"Oh, hello there," the Brownies heard her say. None of them could believe how brave she was being.

"Who's she speaking to?" Ellie wondered.

But before anyone could answer, they saw Sam step back into the lobby again.

"It's OK," said Sam quietly. "We'll look after you."

The Brownies heard the door being locked, then Sam reappeared in the hall. By now, Vicky had turned all the lights back on.

"Is everything OK?" she asked.

"Everything's fine," said Sam. "But it looks like someone wants to gatecrash our sleepover!" She was holding something tightly in her arms.

Vicky hurried over. "Well, goodness gracious me."

The Brownies moved closer to take a look.

"Don't get too close," Sam said. "It might get frightened."

"What is it?" the Brownies asked.

"It's a cat!" declared Charlie. "A sweet little cat!"

"Oh, the poor thing!" said Ellie, quickly forgetting how frightened she'd been of the noise the cat had made before. "Is it all right?"

"It's a bit wet," said Jamila.

"I'll fetch a towel," said Vicky.

"It's probably cold," Molly pointed out, "if it's been outside in this rain and wind."

The cat snuggled into Sam's arms, its eyes wide as it stared timidly at all the Brownies.

"It's probably hungry and thirsty too!" Charlie said.

"Good thinking, Charlie," said Vicky. "Let's find it some food."

The school hall had gone from sleepy and quiet to bustling and busy in a very short space of time. Sam sent some of the girls to look in the Brownie store cupboard for a box or some kind of container that they could use as a cat basket. They returned a few minutes later with a sturdy cardboard box.

"That's perfect," said Sam. "The poor thing hasn't got a collar or a name tag and I think it's too late to find out where it's come from now. We'd better keep it here for the night and then try to discover where it lives in the morning."

Charlie and some of the other Brownies went in search of something the cat could eat. They decided that, as they didn't have any cat food, the best thing to do was put some small pieces of bread into a bowl with a little bit of milk.

When the food was put in front of the cat, it gobbled it up, purring as it ate.

"It was obviously hungry," said Vicky. "Well done for your quick thinking, Brownies."

"Is it all right?" Caitlin asked.

"It seems fine to me," said Sam. "I think

it just got out for the night and couldn't find its way home in the rain."

"Where will it sleep?" asked Ellie.

"I think the best thing would be for us to find a nice warm place next to the radiator in the little room by the kitchen," said Vicky.

Sam lined the box with her fleece jacket. Then she put it in the room with another saucer of food and gently placed the cat inside the box.

Purring, the cat curled into a ball, yawned and went to sleep.

"Aaaaaaaah!" whispered all the Brownies.

"Isn't it sweet?" said Charlie.

Ellie yawned. "Yeah," she said sleepily.

All around her, the other Brownies were yawning too.

"Come on," said Vicky, closing the door and leaving the cat in peace. "I think we all need our sleep, don't we?"

The Brownies climbed back into their sleeping bags and fell, exhausted, to sleep.

The sound of Vicky and Sam's snoring woke the Brownies in the morning.

"Sounds like they don't want to wake up!" joked Jamila, and all the Brownies giggled.

"Come on!" urged Charlie. "Let's get dressed so that we can go and see how the cat is!"

Sam and Vicky were soon woken by the noise of the excited Brownies getting dressed.

"Morning, girls!" Vicky yawned, stretching her arms above her head. "Who's ready for breakfast?"

"Me!" said every Brownie in the hall.

"But we need to check on the cat first!" said Charlie.

"Good point," said Sam. "Come on, then."

"We'd better not frighten it," Charlie warned as everyone made their way to the little room next to the kitchen.

"Oh look!" exclaimed Boo, as they opened the door. "It's awake!"

The little cat raised its head from the box, gave a huge miaow, and then rushed over to say hello to the Brownies.

"Isn't it cute!" said Ashvini.

"Gorgeous," agreed Bethany.

"And it's hungry too!" said Vicky, pointing to the empty food bowl. The cat kept sticking its nose into the bowl and then looking up at them, miaowing impatiently.

"I think we'd better give the cat some more bread and milk," suggested Charlie.

"But what's going to happen to it?" Jamila asked.

"Don't worry," said Sam. "It probably lives
in one of the houses down the road. It's a
good job that none of you are allergic to cats
or we wouldn't have been able to look after it
last night. Still, Vicky and I will find out
where it lives as soon as you all go home after
breakfast."

"Breakfast!" said Megan and Molly at the
same time. "We're starving!"

The other Brownies agreed.

"Come on then," said Sam. "Let's get
cooking! Everyone needs to help!"

Chapter 10

"I was too tired to do anything yesterday," said Ellie at school on Monday.

"Me too," agreed Katie.

"That was just the best sleepover EVER!" said Jamila. "And the show was great, too."

"But do you think that little cat is OK?" wondered Charlie. She'd been thinking about it since Sunday morning.

"I'm sure Vicky and Sam have made sure it's all right," said Jamila, hugging her friend. "Don't worry!"

"Anyway," said Grace. "We'll find out tomorrow because it's Brownies again!"

The following night, Brownies seemed strange without Jessica.

"I wonder who is going to be the new Sixer for the Foxes?" Katie asked her best friends when they arrived.

Secretly, she wished it could be her, but she knew that she hadn't been a Brownie long enough to be made a Sixer already. Most likely, it was going to be Emma, her Seconder, who'd become the new Sixer.

All the Brownies were still full of excitement about the show and sleepover, so when they were called into the Brownie Ring, Sam and Vicky had to hold up their right hands for absolutely ages before they finally fell quiet.

"Goodness gracious me!" Sam said, giggling.

"We thought you'd never stop talking!"

The Brownies giggled too.

"I don't know about you," said Sam, looking around at the Brownies, "but I had a great time at the sleepover."

"Yeeaaaaaaaah!" the Brownies agreed.

"And I thought you were all really terrific in the show too," added Vicky. "You were brilliant – well done! Give yourselves a clap!"

The Brownies laughed some more and clapped to congratulate themselves.

"In fact," said Vicky when the clapping stopped, "you were so good that we've got some badges to hand out!"

The Brownies looked around expectantly.

"Some of you have been working towards being awarded your Entertainer badge and the performances at the show mean you've completed it!" Sam smiled.

"But don't worry if your name isn't called out this evening," said Vicky. "Everything you did at the show will be put towards getting your Entertainer badge soon. There'll be lots of opportunities for you to finish the badge in the next couple of months."

Sam looked down at a piece of paper she had with names on it. "Would Holly, Caitlin, Ashvini, Amy and Poppy like to collect their badges."

The five Brownies went over to Vicky and Sam and, as they were given their badges, each girl held up her right hand in the special Brownie sign.

"Well done, Brownies," said Sam. "Now—"

But before Sam could finish, Charlie shot up her hand and waved it impatiently.

"Yes, Charlie?" said Sam.

"Please, Sam, what happened to the cat?" asked Charlie.

"Yes," said Jamila. "Did you find out where it lived?"

Sam and Vicky looked at each other and then back at the Brownies.

"Actually, we were going to tell you about that," said Vicky. "We tried lots of houses but no one knew the cat or where it lived. So, with no collar or name tag, we had to take the cat to the rescue centre. The people there checked to see if it had a microchip to identify it, but no luck. So, it's being looked after there."

There was a gasp of disappointment from the Brownies.

"The poor cat!" sighed Charlie. "We need to help find its owners!"

"We could do posters!" suggested Ellie. "And put them up in the school."

"And get people in the nearby houses and shops to put them up too!" Jamila added.

"That's a great idea," said Sam. "Why don't we start making them right now."

"Yeaaaay!" agreed the Brownies.

CAT FOUND said the posters. The Brownies did lots of them and made sure that each one gave the details of when and where the cat was found, what it looked like, and where it was now. They even put the telephone number of the rescue centre on them so that the owners could, hopefully, be reunited with their cat quickly.

After the Brownie meeting, all the Brownies took a poster with them to put up near their home. Vicky and Sam said they would make some more copies and ask the local shops to display them in their windows.

The rest of the week was hard for all the 1st Badenbridge Brownies. They saw the posters every time they walked down the street, or went to school. And each time, they wondered if the cat was still at the rescue centre, or if it was sitting cuddled up on its owner's lap…

"Is there any news about the cat?" Charlie asked when she arrived at Brownies the following week.

"Wait until we get together for our Pow Wow!" said Sam, winking.

So there is! thought Charlie. She just hoped the news was good.

After starting the Brownie meeting on their Six tables, drawing, colouring and doing some wordsearches, Sam and Vicky called

everyone over to form a Brownie Ring.
It was time to find out about the cat!

"Now," said Sam, grinning at Charlie.
"I'm aware that some of you are anxious to
know if there is any news of the cat that we
found during our sleepover."

The Brownies sat up expectantly.

"Well, I got a phone call from the rescue
centre yesterday," Sam continued. "The cat's
owners saw our posters and turned up at the
centre. The cat's name is Tigger."

"Aaaaaahhh!" sighed all the Brownies
happily.

"But the extra-special thing is that the
owners told the rescue centre that if they
hadn't seen the posters, they'd never have
found Tigger! So it's all down to your hard
work that they found her," said Sam.

"Yeaaaaaah!" said the Brownies.

"It's a bit of a mystery, you see," added Vicky. "Tigger lives a few miles away. They think she must have hopped into someone's car without being spotted and got a lift here! The owners were looking for her closer to home and it wasn't until they came to the

shops yesterday that they spotted the posters."

Grace stuck up her hand.

"So we did a good turn?" she asked.

"The First Badenbridge Brownies definitely did a good turn." Sam smiled. "Well done, all of you!"

Gathering together later to get ready to play a game, Charlie, Jamila, Grace, Katie and Ellie were talking about the good news they'd just heard.

"Isn't it brilliant about the cat?" said Ellie.

"Yes – I'm so pleased she's back home," agreed Katie.

"She was so sweet," said Grace.

"And so sad when she was all wet and hungry," added Jamila.

"But we Brownies looked after her, didn't we?" said Charlie.

"That's because Brownies are the best!" said Jamila.

"Yessssss!" shouted the five best friends. "Brownies are BRILLIANT!"

How Bethany got her Entertainer badge!

1. Read a poem at the school poetry competition. Played Frère Jacques on my recorder for the other Brownies. Wrote and performed a puppet show about the Roman invasion of Britain. Made costumes for my puppets.

2. Took part in a Brownie Show and planned the make-up and costumes. Made a special programme, listing who was performing, and decorated it with my own drawings.

3. Performed in the show! I also helped to tidy up the hall afterwards, of course!

Are you a Musical Whizz-Kid?

Do you have a fantastic singing voice, or play a really cool instrument? Then why not perform Frère Jacques, just like Bethany did!

Meet all the
1st Badenbridge Brownies!

Jessica

Lottie

Katie

Amber

Emma

Caitlin

Lucy

Grace

Molly

Boo

Collect all the books in the series!

It's the girls' first day at Brownies, and they're all feeling nervous and excited. But their worries are soon forgotten as there's so much to do – decorating bookmarks, singing songs, playing games and making new friends. And soon, the new Brownies must start preparing for their Promise Celebrations!

Perfect Promise

I've got it! ◯

It's Thinking Day – a day to remember Brownies all over the world. The girls have decided to celebrate by finding out all about Brownies in Africa. They're learning special songs and dances, and how to make beautiful African beads – it's time for the Brownies to get creative!

Helping Hands

I've got it! ◯

The Brownies are having a sleepover, and the girls are super-excited! First they're going to put on a show, and then sleep out in the Brownie hall. The girls furiously start practising their performances, but on the night of the show, things don't quite go to plan...

Sleepover Surprise

I've Got it! ◯

Katie and Grace bring their cousin, Sienna, to Brownies. Sienna lives in Australia and she's a Brownie, too! Vicky and Sam, the Brownie Leaders, suggest the girls might like to do their World guiding badge and find out more about Brownies in other countries. The girls can't wait to get started!

Friends Forever

I've Got it! ◯

Join the Brownies

Brownies do it all!

They do cool things to get badges like the Artist badge and the Computer badge, they have sleepovers, they make heaps of friends and have lots of fun.

Brownies are aged from seven to ten and are part of Girlguiding UK, the largest organisation for girls and young women in the UK, which has around 575,000 members.

To learn more about what Brownies get up to, visit www.girlguiding.org.uk/brownies or call 0800 169 5901 to find out how you can join in the fun.